W9-BMB-735

Sometimes there is a happening in our lives that changes the way we think about ourselves and sends us along a new path. These turning points can come when we are young—through a person we meet, an experience we have, a difficulty we overcome.

Since 1789, only forty-two people have been president of the United States. What has made these forty-two people unique? Was there a turning point in their young lives that caused them to change direction and set them on a path that led them to the White House?

—Judith St. George

With love to Peter. —*J.St.G.*

Dedicated to my family, extended and immediate. Without their unwavering support, nothing would have been possible. —*B.S.*

Patricia Lee Gauch, editor

PHILOMEL BOOKS A division of Penguin Young Readers Group. Published by The Penguin Group.
Penguin Group (USA) Inc., 375 Hudson Street, New York, NY 10014, U.S.A. Penguin Group (Canada), 90 Eglinton Avenue East, Suite 700, Toronto, Ontario, Canada M4P 2Y3 (a division of Pearson Penguin Canada Inc.). Penguin Books Ltd, 80 Strand, London WC2R 0RL, England. Penguin Ireland, 25 St. Stephen's Green, Dublin 2, Ireland (a division of Penguin Books Ltd.). Penguin Group (Australia), 250 Camberwell Road, Camberwell, Victoria 3124, Australia (a division of Pearson Australia Group Pty Ltd). Penguin Books India Pvt Ltd, 11 Community Centre, Panchsheel Park, New Delhi - 110 017, India. Penguin Group (NZ), Cnr Airborne and Rosedale Roads, Albany, Auckland 1310, New Zealand (a division of Pearson New Zealand Ltd). Penguin Books (South Africa) (Pty) Ltd, 24 Sturdee Avenue, Rosebank, Johannesburg 2196, South Africa. Penguin Books Ltd, Registered Offices: 80 Strand, London WC2R 0RL, England.

Published simultaneously in Canada. Manufactured in China by South China Printing Co. Ltd.

Design by Semadar Megged. The illustrations were done in mixed media including watercolor, gouache, and ink on Arches watercolor paper. The text is set in 15.5 point Dante.

Library of Congress Cataloging-in-Publication Data
St. George, Judith, 1931– Make your mark, Franklin Roosevelt / Judith St. George ; illustrated by Britt Spencer.
p. cm. Includes bibliographical references.
1. Roosevelt, Franklin D. (Franklin Delano), 1882–1945—Childhood and youth—Juvenile literature. 2. Presidents—United States—Biography—Juvenile literature. I. Spencer, Britt. II. Title. E807.S79 2007 973.917092—dc22 2006008921

ISBN 978-0-399-24175-8 10 9 8 7 6 5 4 3 2 1
First Impression

JUDITH ST. GEORGE

illustrated by

BRITT SPENCER

Make Your Mark, FRANKLIN ROOSEVELT

Philomel Books

Chapter 1. Franklin and Mama

Tall, beautiful Sara Delano Roosevelt gave birth to her only child at home on January 30, 1882. Home was Springwood, a large wooded estate above the Hudson River near Hyde Park, New York. What should Sara and her husband, James, name their baby? Sara was fond of her uncle Franklin and she adored her family, the Delanos. Franklin Delano Roosevelt it was.

Right from the start, Franklin was the center of his mother's world. Why, until he was three, she called him "Baby." And Sara was definite about what she wanted. She wanted her darling boy in dresses, so dresses it was. And she doted on his long golden curls, so curls it was. But Franklin was definite about what he wanted, too, and by six he wanted the curls off. Off they came!

Sara and young Franklin became fast companions—reading books together and riding to church in the family carriage. But sometimes Sara was out doing "good deeds"—seeing that flowers, food and clothing were sent to shut-ins and the poor. When she was gone, she left Franklin with a nursemaid. He didn't like that one bit.

What Franklin did like was standing with his mother by the family Christmas tree at Christmastime, doing his own "good deeds," handing out games and toys to the children of Springwood workers. He probably knew he would receive lots of gifts later himself—and he did.

Both Sara and James came from wealthy families, the French Delanos and the Dutch Roosevelts. Being wealthy meant Sara, James and Franklin didn't have just one home, they had three. They lived at Springwood during spring and fall, in a vacation home in Campobello, Canada, during summers and in a New York City apartment winters, with trips to Europe almost every year.

Franklin traveled often with his parents and wherever they went, he was always Sara's darling boy. During one voyage to Europe, rough seas smashed a bulkhead. Water poured into the Roosevelts' cabin. The ship was sinking! Sara wrapped Franklin in her fur coat. "Poor little boy," she cried, "if he must go down, he is going down warm."

Just then, Franklin saw his favorite toy float across the cabin floor. "Mama! Mama! Save my jumping jack!" he pleaded.

Wading through the water, she did. (The ship didn't sink.)

Two years later, five-year-old Franklin visited the White House with his parents. President Grover Cleveland patted Franklin's head. "My little man," he said, "I am making a strange wish for you. It is that you may never be president of the United States."

Why not? Didn't presidents live in a grand white house, and didn't everyone know who they were?

But Sara was horrified. Good gracious, her darling boy in politics? Why, she was "keeping Franklin's mind on nice things," and politics weren't nice. Politics meant appearing in public places. Politics meant begging for votes from all sorts of people. No, what Sara wished for Franklin was that he grow up to live at Springwood as a country gentleman—just like his father.

Chapter 2. Franklin and Popsy

Before he was six, Franklin was hooked on reading. He could write, too: "we coasted!" he wrote to his parents, "yesterday nothing dangerous yet, look out for tomorrow!! (signed) your boy. F." Such a tease!

Franklin didn't go to public school. My, no, James and Sara had governesses teach him at home. He even learned German from a neighbor's German governess.

James Roosevelt didn't care much for books or reading. Instead, he raised trotting horses. James, whose first wife had died, was almost twice Sara's age. Though he was old enough to be Franklin's grandfather, it didn't matter to Franklin. As a young boy, he called his beloved father Popsy. They were Best Pals.

Franklin wasn't even two when James first took him sledding on the steep hill behind their house. That was just the beginning. Popsy taught Franklin to fish, row, ice-skate, snowshoe, toboggan, even sail an iceboat on the frozen Hudson River. Sometimes on their Canadian vacations, Popsy let Franklin take the wheel of his yacht.

What a thrill! Franklin liked sailing best.

Riding was a close second. James offered Franklin a pony, Debby, and a red setter dog, Marksman, IF he would groom and feed them faithfully. You bet he would. He promised he'd do just as good a job as Popsy's stable hands, and he did.

But one fall day James led a foxhunt at Springwood. Franklin followed on Debby. Just as the hunters closed in on the fox, Franklin galloped up. James was angry at Franklin—not for spoiling the hunt, but because he'd run Debby too hard.

Popsy often asked Franklin to go along with him in the horse and buggy. And the two of them rode out on their horses almost every day to check on the barns, stables, gardens, dairy, greenhouses, fields . . . and trees. James taught his son all about elms, oaks, maples and more.

CLEVELAND WINS!
GROVER

Franklin learned something else. His father was important. As his father's son, he was important, too. When his father (Mr. James) and he (Master Franklin) rode by, Springwood workers tipped their caps politely.

James was often urged to run for office, both in New York State and Washington. He always refused. Gentlemen didn't go into politics. But one night young Franklin was awakened by drums and flutes playing "Yankee Doodle Dandy." He ran down to the porch in his nightgown. Wagons lined the driveway. Men carried torches. Grover Cleveland had been elected president for a second term. Franklin never forgot that "perfectly grand evening."

Franklin loved to play with his nephew and niece, Taddy and Helen, who lived right next door to Springwood. Franklin had one good friend, Edmund Rogers. Though Franklin was shy, he also liked to be in charge. His mother once scolded him for being bossy.

"Mummie," he said, "if I didn't give orders, nothing would happen."

Franklin didn't have to share his parents with brothers or sisters. No schoolyard bullies picked on him. He was never spanked. (Once, when he was naughty, his father said, "Franklin, consider yourself spanked.") The butler, maids, nursemaid, housekeeper, laundress and cook doted on Franklin . . . and spoiled him.

Franklin enjoyed his sunny, pleasant, pampered life. Why shouldn't he? He was surrounded by all the love and attention any boy could hope for. He was the center of his small world, and that was fine with him.

Chapter 3. Franklin on His Own

Franklin was scared. His papa was in bed with a heart attack! Was he going to die? James Roosevelt didn't die. But his life changed. Sara told Franklin that his father could no longer play sports with him. Papa's life must be quiet and worry-free.

Franklin was on his own.

A doctor advised James to take the mineral springs in Nauheim, Germany, for his health. Franklin spent five long summers there with his mother and father. The other guests were all sick or old. They bathed in the mineral springs. They ate plain food. They read.

It was so boring!

But Franklin didn't complain. That would worry his father. He sailed his toy yacht on the pond . . . by himself. He played Indian with his bow and arrow . . . by himself. A family friend gave him swimming lessons by tying a rope around his waist and throwing him into the pool again and again. Each time Franklin was yanked out, he was half-drowned. His parents soon put a stop to that.

Back at Springwood, Franklin still didn't complain. But he knew how to get his own way. On Sundays he sometimes had a headache. That meant no church. Papa called it "Franklin's Sunday headache." If he had a sore finger, the piano or drawing lesson was called off. Was he ever scolded? No.

But if it was something serious, Franklin never said a word. Once a steel rod fell on his head while he was traveling on James's private train. Franklin didn't say anything. He just pulled on a cap so that his papa wouldn't see the bloody gash.

Governesses came and went at Springwood. Franklin's French governess, high-spirited Jeanne Sandoz, had a conscience. She taught more than French. She tried to teach Franklin about the lives of the poor and helpless. Did he learn anything? Maybe. In a report on Egypt, he wrote: "The working people had nothing . . . The kings made them work so hard and gave them so little that by wingo! they nearly starved and by jinks! they had hardly any clothes so they died in quadrillions."

Without Papa as a playmate, Franklin became a collector, first stamps and then, when James gave him a shotgun, birds.

Loving the sea as he did, Franklin collected sea yarns, yachting books, naval pictures and histories. He and Edmund Rogers sailed a ship on unknown waters—in the crow's nest of their tree house. They even built a raft and launched it on the banks of the wide Hudson River. (It sank.)

But Franklin knew how to entertain himself. He knew how to act cheerful, no matter what. He knew how to please adults. But what did he know about the world outside of Hyde Park or the rough-and-tumble world of boys his own age? Nothing. He would soon begin to learn about both. Franklin was off to boarding school. His mother and father had been his models. Now he was about to meet a formidable new one.

S.S
ROOSEV

Chapter 4. Franklin and the Rector

Groton School seemed like a long way from Springwood. Franklin had lots of questions. Would he fit in? Who would be his friends? Would the work be hard?

September 15, 1896, was the big arrival day. Four brick buildings sat on a Massachusetts hillside leading down to a river. What a surprise! It looked just like the countryside back home. Franklin's room was a surprise, too. It had only a bed, bureau and chair, with a curtain for a door and pegs instead of a closet. It looked more like a cell.

A tall, blond man with broad shoulders greeted Franklin with a good, strong handshake—the headmaster. Franklin had to look up, up, up at the Reverend Endicott Peabody, known as the Rector. As the Rector's piercing blue eyes took his measure, Franklin felt small and puny.

ROOS

First things first—make friends. The boys in Franklin's class had started Groton at twelve. Not Franklin. Because his parents didn't want to lose their "darling boy," they kept Franklin home until he was fourteen. Groton friendships had been made. Leaders were already chosen.

From his very first day, Franklin was an outsider.

Franklin knew he'd have to make it on his own, but he didn't want to worry his parents. "I am getting on finely both mentally and physically," he wrote home.

Despite what new-boy Franklin wrote, he quickly found out the old-boys played rough. They mocked him for the accent he'd picked up in Europe. They mocked him for his bow to Mrs. Peabody at their good-night handshake. They mocked him for always being on time and eager in class.

Franklin soon figured out that sports were the way to make it at Groton. The Rector had every boy play football to develop "manly Christian character." That was a problem. Franklin had never played football or even been on a team. Besides, he was only five foot three inches tall and weighed one hundred pounds. He made the seventh team out of eight.

As for baseball, Franklin got stuck on the BBBs—the Bum Baseball Boys team.

Franklin also figured out it was important to have the Groton "tone." To be just like his classmates, he worked hard on his "tone." He cheered loudly at football games. He sledded and skated. Along with everyone else, he complained about the food, the twice-a-day cold showers and the constant clanging of bells.

Getting a black mark meant being one of the boys. At last Franklin earned one. "I am very glad of it as I was thought to have no school spirit before," he proudly wrote home.

Franklin was beginning to fit in.

As for the Rector, Franklin came to love AND fear him. The Rector's 110 boys were his family. Every day he strode across the campus, greeting each boy by name, stopping to chat, talking sports with the athletes. But he could be strict, too. One of Franklin's classmates got six black marks. The Rector glared at him. "Are you looking for trouble, boy? Well, here I am!"

Franklin admired the Rector. How forceful he was, pacing behind his desk in class or pounding on his Sunday pulpit! And Franklin heard over and over the Rector preach—go out and serve the world . . . serve other people, the church and especially our country, maybe as governors or senators.

Franklin would do anything to please the Rector. Every day he went to morning church services and evening prayers. Helping others? He'd do that, too . . . someday. But politics? His parents said gentlemen didn't go into politics. No, much as Franklin wanted to please the Rector, politics weren't for him.

Chapter 5. Franklin and Cousin Theodore

If the Rector wanted his boys to serve the world, he knew they'd better learn what was going on in the world. Having them argue against one another in fierce school debates was one way to learn. Franklin was a good debater.

Why shouldn't he be? His parents always encouraged him to speak up and express his opinions at the dinner table, and he did.

The Rector invited guest speakers to talk about their worlds. Reformer Jacob Riis described New York City slums. Educator Booker T. Washington told about his Virginia childhood as a slave. It was a lot for Franklin to take in. Had his governesses ever taught him that much about city slums or what it meant to be a slave? No.

One day Franklin's fifth cousin, Theodore Roosevelt, came to Groton. An energetic, rugged man of action, Cousin Theodore marched vigorously across the stage and thrilled the boys with his tales of being a New York City police commissioner.

Franklin was so proud that he felt ten feet tall.

After his speech, Cousin Theodore had a friendly chat with Franklin. Could Franklin come to his family's Fourth of July celebration on Long Island? It would be a bully party. But Sara heard about the invitation and refused—in her son's name.

For once, Franklin stood up to his mother. "Please don't make any more arrangements for my future happiness," he wrote, and off he went to Long Island.

In April 1898, the country was plunged into the Spanish-American War and the world turned topsy-turvy. Sixteen-year-old Franklin turned topsy-turvy, too. Though the Rector's latest school report described him as "a good boy," Franklin was tired of being a "good boy." It was time he became a rugged man of action like Cousin Theodore. Franklin plotted with two friends to hide in the pieman's cart, travel to Boston and sign up in the navy.

Before Franklin could escape, he fell sick with a sore throat and red rash. Scarlet fever! His parents rushed up to Groton. But no visitors were allowed in the school hospital. That didn't stop Sara Roosevelt. With her long skirts and hat in place, she perched on a ladder to talk with her "darling boy" through his hospital window.

In the fall of 1898, Cousin Theodore ran for governor of New York. He won.

What rip-roaring good news! Franklin wrote home that the dormitory was "wild with delight." So was he.

In January 1899, Franklin and his parents boarded James's private railroad car for Albany to hear Cousin Theodore give his first speech as governor. Franklin sat with his parents in the balcony of the Albany State Capitol. He was sure that Cousin Theodore would give a humdinger of a speech, and he did.

"If a man has courage, goodness, and brains, no limit can be placed to the greatness of the work he may accomplish," the new governor told his audience. "He is the man needed today in politics."

Why, Cousin Theodore sounded just like the Rector! What was all this about gentlemen not going into politics? Look at Cousin Theodore. He was a politician *and* a gentleman. He had courage, goodness, and brains as well. He was exactly the kind of man the Rector was always talking about.

Chapter 6. Franklin and the World

Groton became Franklin's home away from home. His father had grown very weak and his mother seldom left his side. Sixteen-year-old Franklin admired Cousin Theodore, but the Rector and Mrs. Peabody were right there for him. He looked forward to "Mrs. Peabody's Parlor" every week, and talks with the Rector about religion and everything else under the sun were like the man-to-man talks he used to have with his papa. Franklin began to understand—and take to heart—the Rector's passion for moving out into the world.

Joining the Episcopal Church spurred Franklin on. He taught Sunday school. The church choir needed a bass? He stepped forward. Local churches needed an organist? Franklin stepped forward.

The Rector had founded a camp for boys from the Boston slums. Franklin wasn't much at football, but he was a whiz at sailing, canoeing and swimming. He pitched in and taught water sports for two summer sessions.

Mrs. Freeman, an elderly black widow, became Franklin's special concern. He and a Groton classmate made sure she had heat and food and shoveled her out when it snowed. Franklin grew fond of her and called her "a dear old thing."

College loomed. Franklin dreamed of going to Annapolis. He'd become a naval officer and spend his life at sea. But his father wouldn't hear of it. Groton men went to Harvard. Franklin didn't argue with his ailing papa.

In his fourth and last year, Franklin finally was a Groton "old boy." Six feet tall, with pesky braces off his teeth, he was delighted to look older at last. But he needed glasses. His choice? Pince-nez glasses like Cousin Theodore's, of course.

Although Franklin never made it in sports, he starred in the senior play. Wearing his father's old tuxedo and top hat, he played a country bumpkin, Uncle Bopaddy. Being on stage was the best. In the limelight! Getting laughs!

Suddenly it was June 1900 . . . and graduation. Franklin won the Latin Prize. "You may imagine I feel rather tickled," he confessed. The Rector's final report? "He has been a thoroughly faithful scholar & a most satisfactory member of this school throughout his course. I part with Franklin with reluctance."

Eighteen-year-old Franklin parted from the Rector and Mrs. Peabody with reluctance, too. "I feel awfully to be leaving here for good," he told his parents.

Franklin later called the Rector's "guiding hand" and "inspiring example" among the blessings of his life. Looking back on his Groton days, he never forgot how the Reverend Endicott Peabody had unlocked his mind and heart to the outside world—to helping others and serving his country with honor.

And serve his country he did. In the years ahead, Franklin followed his cousin Theodore Roosevelt into politics. Cousin Theodore was assistant secretary of the navy. So was Franklin. Cousin Theodore was governor of New York. So was Franklin. Cousin Theodore was president of the United States. So was Franklin Delano Roosevelt.

Franklin Delano Roosevelt was born on his family's estate in Hyde Park, New York, on January 30, 1882. As the only child of wealthy and privileged parents, he was educated by private tutors. After four years at the Groton School, Roosevelt went on to Harvard and Columbia Law School.

An admirer of his fifth cousin, Republican President Teddy Roosevelt, Franklin Roosevelt entered politics as a Democrat and won a New York State Senate seat in 1910. During World War I, he served as assistant secretary of the navy.

In 1921, after swimming in icy Canadian waters, Roosevelt was felled by polio, paralyzing him from the chest down. But he kept going. With braces, a cane and a strong arm to lean on, he became governor of New York in 1928.

In 1932, when the country was in the depths of the Great Depression and twenty-five percent of American workers were jobless, Roosevelt became the thirty-second president of the United States. "The only thing we have to fear is fear itself," he said in his Inaugural Address, and he took his own advice.

Roosevelt pushed through Congress his New Deal—social programs to bring relief to the unemployed, aid to help businesses and agriculture recover, and loans to those losing their homes. Establishing new agencies, he convinced Congress to pass Social Security, higher taxes, work-relief programs and controls over banks and public utilities.

In 1940 Roosevelt became the first president in history to run for, and win, a third term. When the United States entered World War II in 1941, victory became his main concern. Shortly after he was sworn in for a fourth term, sixty-two-year-old Roosevelt died on April 12, 1945.

During his twelve years in office, Franklin Delano Roosevelt, who set out to enrich and improve American life everywhere, left behind a legacy of the most sweeping social changes in the country's history.

BIBLIOGRAPHY

Alsop, Joseph. *FDR, 1882–1945: A Centenary Remembrance.* New York: The Viking Press, 1982.

Ashburn, Frank D. *Peabody of Groton: A Portrait.* New York: Coward McCann, Inc., 1944.

Burns, James MacGregor. *Roosevelt: The Lion and the Fox.* New York: Harcourt, Brace and Company, 1956.

Davis, Kenneth S. *FDR: The Beckoning of Destiny, 1882–1928, a History.* New York: G. P. Putnam's Sons, 1971.

Freidel, Frank. *Franklin D. Roosevelt: The Apprenticeship.* Boston: Little, Brown and Company, 1952.

Kintrea, Frank. "'Old Peabo' and the School." *American Heritage* 31, no. 6 (October/November 1980): 98–105.

Kleeman, Rita Halle. *Gracious Lady: The Life of Sara Delano Roosevelt.* New York: D. Appleton-Century Company, 1935.

Miller, Nathan. *FDR: An Intimate History.* Garden City, New York: Doubleday & Company, Inc., 1983.

Morgan, Ted. *FDR: A Biography.* New York: Simon and Schuster, 1985.

Morris, Edmund. *The Rise of Theodore Roosevelt.* New York: Coward, McCann & Geoghegan, Inc., 1979.

Roosevelt, Elliott, ed. *F.D.R.: His Personal Letters—Early Years.* New York: Duell, Sloan and Pearce, 1947.

Roosevelt, Sara Delano. *My Boy Franklin.* New York: Ray Long & Richard Smith, Inc., 1933.

Steeholm, Clara, and Hardy Steeholm. *The House at Hyde Park.* New York: The Viking Press, 1950.

Ward, Geoffrey C. *Before the Trumpet: Young Franklin Roosevelt, 1882–1905.* New York: Harper & Row, Publishers, 1985.

Ward, Geoffrey C. "The House at Hyde Park." *American Heritage* 38, no. 3 (April 1987): 41–50.